Happy Birthday, America

Mary Pope Osborne   Illustrated by Peter Catalanotto

A Deborah Brodie Book
ROARING BROOK PRESS
New Milford, Connecticut

A Deborah Brodie Book   Published by Roaring Brook Press   Roaring Brook Press is a division of Holtzbrinck
Publishing Holdings Limited Partnership   143 West Street, New Milford, Connecticut 06776   All rights reserved
Distributed in Canada by H. B. Fenn and Company, Ltd.

Library of Congress Cataloging-in-Publication Data

Osborne, Mary Pope.   Happy birthday, America / Mary Pope Osborne ; illustrated by Peter Catalanotto.   p. cm.
Summary: The whole family joins in a lively small-town celebration of Independence Day, including a parade, a picnic,
music, and fireworks. An author's note explains the origin of the celebration of July 4th.
[1. Fourth of July—Fiction.   2. Family life—Fiction.]   I. Catalanotto, Peter, ill.   II. Title.
PZ7.O91167 Hap 2003   [E]—dc21   2002009698
ISBN 0-7613-1675-2 (hardcover)   ISBN 1-59643-051-6 (paperback)

Roaring Brook Press books are available for special promotions and premiums.
For details, contact: Director of Special Markets, Holtzbrinck Publishers.

Book design by Jennifer Browne   Printed in the United States of America

(hardcover) 10 9 8 7 6 5 4 3 2 1   (paperback) 10 9 8 7 6 5 4 3 2 1

On the Fourth of July,
Mom, Dad, Katie,
Grandpa, Grandma,
Aunt Beth, baby Jess,
our dog, Bud, and I
go to Memorial Park.

We march around the ball field
in the Pet Parade.
I play a kazoo.
Katie waves red, white, and blue streamers.

Bud touches noses
with a pig on a leash.

From noon till two, I sell popcorn and pizza
at the Pee Wee Football booth.
"Fifty cents a bag!"
"Hot, hot, hot, a dollar a slice!"

Grandma sells raffle tickets
for the American Legion Squadron 242.
"A dollar a chance
to win a hand-knit colonial flag!"

Grandpa wears his old fishing cap.
He sits in his wheelchair,
while on the bandstand,
Katie tap-dances the Hornpipe Boogie
in a sailor suit
with Miss Cindy's School of Dance.
Aunt Beth gets so excited,
she dances, too.

I go with Grandpa and Dad
to see the antique cars.
We pitch pennies at the Kiwanis booth.
I win a blue bunny
and give it to Jess.

Under a tree
high school kids paint Katie's face
with stars.
Katie and I have a sword fight
with balloons.

Firemen from five different towns
fight water battles
before the sun goes down.

Mom and I buy barbecued chicken
cooked on big racks
by the Knights of Columbus.
We have ice cream and waffles,
then spread out our blankets
for the Concert-Under-the-Stars.
Jess crawls away,
but I bring him back.

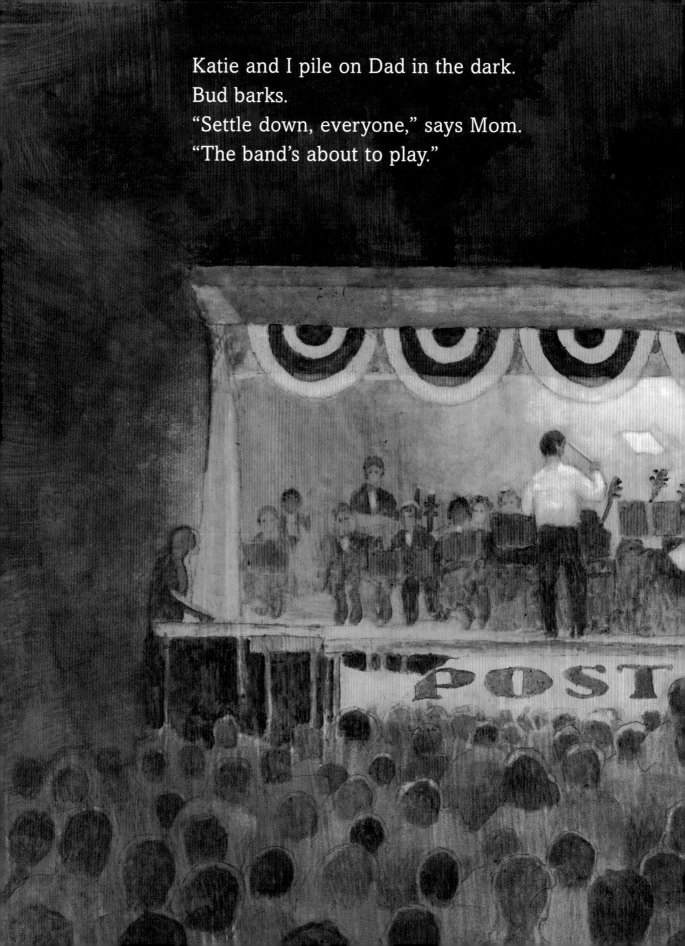

Katie and I pile on Dad in the dark.
Bud barks.
"Settle down, everyone," says Mom.
"The band's about to play."

The conductor wears a red bow tie
and waves a baton.
During "Yankee Doodle,"
his music blows away,
but he waves on.

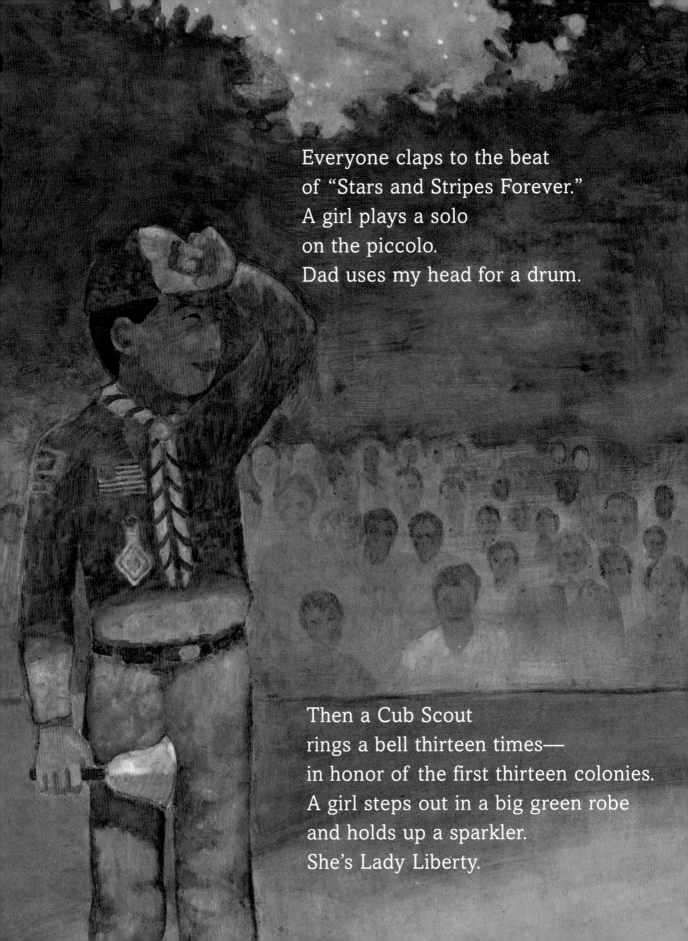

Everyone claps to the beat
of "Stars and Stripes Forever."
A girl plays a solo
on the piccolo.
Dad uses my head for a drum.

Then a Cub Scout
rings a bell thirteen times—
in honor of the first thirteen colonies.
A girl steps out in a big green robe
and holds up a sparkler.
She's Lady Liberty.

Then Mr. Sabertini reads from the Declaration of Independence.

Then we sing "The Star-Spangled Banner,"
and when we get to "the home of the brave,"
the first fireworks go off.
They light the sky—a red-and-blue umbrella.
Bud barks.
Jess cries.

"There they go!"
"Oooooh!" "Ahhhh!" "Wow!"
"Like a palm tree!"
"Like tadpoles!"
"Like a weeping willow!"
"Look how pretty, Jess," says Grandpa,
his first words all day.

A moment of silence.
Then huge bursts of light,
one on top of the other,
and a million pieces of gold
rain down on the trees
near the flag that is still there.

"It's over now, that's it."
We pack up to leave
and walk back to the parking lot
with the crowd.

Dad hums "Yankee Doodle"
as he gets out his keys.
Katie catches a lightning bug,
but lets it go.
"Fly home, Sparky," she says, "to bed."

Jess sleeps all the way back.
So does Grandpa, with Bud on his lap.
I look up at the sky and whisper,
"Happy birthday, America.
Happy Fourth of July."

Then I blow out the stars,
as if they were candles
on a giant birthday cake.

About This Book

On July 4th, 1776, the Declaration of Independence was adopted by the congress of the thirteen colonies of the United States. This occasion marked the birth of America as a free and independent nation.

A year later, on July 4th, the people of Philadelphia celebrated America's birthday with parades, music, and firework displays. "Thus may the 4th of July, that glorious and ever memorable day, be celebrated through America…" said a Virginia newspaper editor, "from age to age, till time shall be no more."

So far, that editor's wish has come true: Since 1776, July 4th has become one of America's most cherished holidays. And today's celebrations still have many elements of the earliest ones. This book was inspired by a recent 4th of July that my husband and I spent in a town in southeastern Pennsylvania. It was also a day made up of many small things— lemon ices, pitch penny, family chat. But it was a day about big things— community, freedom, and pride in our country's history. It truly was a "glorious and ever memorable" celebration of America's birthday.

—Mary Pope Osborne